Franklin and the Little Sisters

Kids Can Press

FRANKLIN and his friends always had lots of fun together. They even had their own cool-io tree fort. One day, they decided to decorate it with their favorite things.

"Bear and I are going over to the tree fort now, Mom," said Franklin. "Everyone is waiting for us."

"Okay, Franklin," said Mrs. Turtle, who was busy picking berries with Dr. Bear.

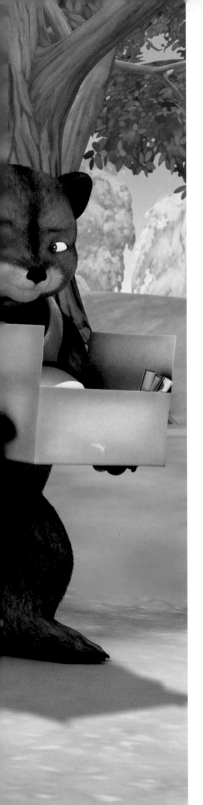

As Franklin and Bear started walking to the fort, they heard giggling behind them.

"Franklin, I think we have company," whispered Bear.

Franklin turned around. Harriet and Beatrice were following them!

"Harriet, we're doing big kid stuff today," said Franklin. "You need to stay with Mom."

"But I want to go to the tree fort," said Harriet.

"Me, too!" said Beatrice.

Bear looked at Franklin. "What are we going to do?"

"I know what to do," said Franklin. "Mom!" he shouted. "Can you please tell Harriet and Beatrice to stay with you and Dr. Bear?"

"Actually," said Mrs. Turtle, "it would be nice if you and Bear watched the girls while we finish picking berries."

"Yay! Tree fort!" cheered Harriet and Beatrice.

"But we were going to put our stuff in the tree fort," Franklin said.

"There will still be time for that," said Mrs. Turtle. "Right now, you need to find something to do with your sisters — something safe. That means on the ground, Franklin."

Franklin's shoulders slumped.

"Okay, Mom," said Franklin. "Let's go, Harriet. Come on, Bea."

When they got to the tree fort, Franklin and Bear decided to take turns watching the girls.

"You first, Franklin!" said Bear, as he ran up the stairs to join their friends.

Franklin sighed.

"We want to go in the tree fort, too," said Harriet.

"Yeah, Franklin," Beatrice added.

"You're too little," said Franklin. "You heard what Mom said. We need to find you something to do on the ground."

Franklin tried to think of a way to keep the girls busy. He looked into his box and got an idea.

"Why don't we paint pictures for the tree fort?" he said, placing the art supplies on the ground.

"Yay! Let's paint!" said Harriet and Beatrice together, grabbing paintbrushes.

"I want red!" said Harriet.

"I want purple!" said Beatrice.

As Franklin watched the girls paint, he heard his friends laughing in the fort. It just wasn't fair! Everyone was having fun except him.

"Harriet, I'm going into the tree fort for a second," said Franklin. "Call if you need me."

"Okay," said Harriet.

Inside the tree fort, Franklin's friends were busy decorating.

"Cool-io!" said Franklin. "Everything looks awesome."

"Thanks," said Goose.

Bear was hanging a picture.

"Come on, Bear. It's your turn to watch the girls."

Bear groaned. "Oh, all right," he said, taping the picture to the wall.

Franklin and Bear climbed back down together.
"Look," said Harriet, holding up her painting. "It's the tree fort."
"Good work," said Bear. "I like the colors."

"Let's go inside and put up our painting!" said Harriet, starting toward the steps. Bea was right behind her.

"You can't go up there, Harriet," said Franklin. "It's not safe."

"Only older kids are allowed," added Bear.

Harriet scowled. "No fair, Franklin," she said.

Beatrice crossed her arms. "No fair, Bear," she said.

"They really want to go into the fort," Bear whispered to Franklin.

"I know," said Franklin. "So do I!"

"What should we do?" said Bear.

"Too bad the fort wasn't on the ground," Bear said.

"That's a great idea!" said Franklin. "Why didn't I think of that?"

Bear looked puzzled. "I hope you're not planning to move our tree fort," he said.

"Of course not. But we can make a new fort with cardboard boxes!" said Franklin.

"There are lots of empty boxes in the tree fort," said Bear. "I'll go get them."

Bear went back into the tree fort and started to lower all the empty boxes with a pulley.

When they had enough boxes, the big brothers and little sisters went to work. Franklin and Bear built a tower. Harriet and Beatrice made some tunnels. Together, they made a cool-io ground fort.

"It still needs something," said Franklin, when they were finished.
"But what?" asked Bear.
"I know," said Harriet. "Paint!"
"Great idea!" said Franklin.

Franklin and Bear were having so much fun painting that they
didn't notice the girls ducking into the ground fort.

"What do you think, Harriet?" asked Franklin.

"Isn't this the most colorful ground fort ever?" asked Bear.

But there was no answer. Harriet and Beatrice were gone!

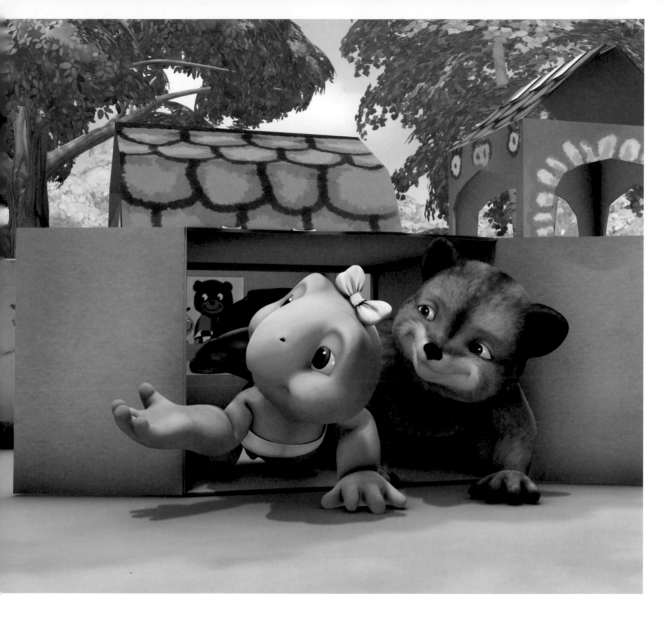

"Uh-oh," said Bear. "Where did they go?"
Suddenly, two heads poked out of the fort.
"Come inside," said Harriet.
"See what we did!" said Beatrice.
Franklin and Bear couldn't believe their eyes!

"Hey, there's my picture on the wall!" said Bear.

"And there's my soccer medal and ball cap!" said Franklin.

"Do you like it?" asked Harriet and Beatrice together.

"It's super cool-io!" said Franklin.

"Good. Because it's your fort, too!" said Harriet.

"Thanks!" said Franklin. "You're the most cool-io little sisters ever!"